GREAT MINDS THINK ALIKE!

By Tex Huntley
Based on the screenplay by Lauren Shell
Illustrated by Erik Doescher

A Random House PICTUREBACK® Book
Random House 🏠 New York

One day in the park, Gabi was reading a story to Susie, Angelica, and the rest of the Reading Rangers. It was about a girl with special powers.

"'The girl concentrated and told her mind to move the apples,'" Gabi read. "'And they started to fall to the ground, one by one.'"

The Rangers were amazed, especially Angelica.

"Gabi, can you really move things with your mind?" Angelica asked. "Or is that just a story?"

"Some people say you can," Gabi replied.

Just then, the ice cream truck rolled up. The kids ran to it—except Angelica. She wanted to go home and see if she had special powers.

Later, Angelica was focusing on a bowl of oranges in her kitchen when Susie walked in.

"Whatcha doing?" Susie asked.

"I'm concentraining," Angelica replied. "I'm about to move those oranges with my mind. Like in the story."

Angelica extended her arms, closed her eyes, and hummed.

"See?" Angelica said, pointing at an orange. "That one moved!"

"Nuh-uh!" Susie said. "It's a special power. You have to be special to do it."

Susie decided to give it a try. Angelica showed her the right way to concentrate.

While Susie and Angelica hummed with their eyes closed, Grandpa Lou walked into the kitchen.

"Aww, they're meditating," he said, taking an orange. As he left, some oranges fell out of the bowl and rolled onto the floor.

The girls opened their eyes, then shouted, "WE DID IT!"

Then Angelica added, "Well, prolly my mind moved most of them, since I go to preschool."

"No," Susie said. "We moved them *together.*"

"Okay," Angelica said. "We did it together. That means our special powers only work if we stay together."

Susie and Angelica went to see what else they could move.

They saw some shirts under Spike, closed their eyes, and focused their powers. Just then, Didi came in and picked up the shirts to make a quilt, then left.

Angelica and Susie opened their eyes and saw that the shirts were gone.

"We did it again!" they exclaimed.

"This means we're going to be famous," Angelica said. "'Presenting: Angelica and Susie Moving Stuff!'"

"Or what about 'Presenting: Susie and Angelica Moving Stuff,'" Susie suggested.

"I should go first because I'm older," Angelica said. "We'll figure out the details later."

Angelica and Susie needed to test their powers in front of an audience. They went to the backyard, where the babies were.

"Me and Susie are going to do a show," Angelica announced.

Susie jumped in front of Angelica. "We'll move something special with our minds! No hands!"

They took Chuckie's Reptar doll and placed it on the edge of the sandbox. They closed their eyes and started to hum.

"Reptar likes it when I hum to him," Chuckie said.

Everyone watched Reptar, so no one noticed when Stu ran into the backyard, frantically looking for his favorite old T-shirts. He accidentally bumped the sandbox, knocking the doll onto the ground.

The babies gasped. Angelica and Susie jumped for joy. Chuckie grabbed his doll. "Are you okay, Reptar?"

"We hafta show Gabi at Reading Rangers tomorrow," Susie declared.
"I was thinking the 'zact same thing," Angelica said. "Let's go talk
about the sparkly costumes we'll wear at our show, partner."

The next day at the park, Angelica and Susie stood in front of the Reading Rangers, ready to show their powers. But what would they concentrate on?

Just then, the ice cream truck rolled through the park.

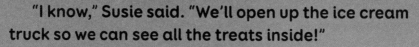

"I know," Susie said. "We'll open up the ice cream truck so we can see all the treats inside!"

The partners closed their eyes, raised their hands, and hummed.

Everyone watched and waited.

The ice cream truck rolled past them. It didn't open.
It didn't even stop.
The Reading Rangers started to cry.
"Don't worry," Gabi said. "It's not time for ice cream
yet. It'll come back."

"Our minds must be more powderful than we thought," Angelica said with amazement. "This is too much 'sponsitility. We've got to quit!"

"Are you sure?" Susie asked.

"It's over," Angelica announced. "I'm going back to being me, and you hafta go back to being a normal boring baby with no special powers."

"I guess so," Susie said. "I'll just have to keep working on my X-ray vision."

"You don't have X-ray vision," Angelica said.

Susie scanned the babies. "Phil, is that a box of gummy worms I see in your diaper?"

It was! The babies were amazed . . . even Angelica. She ran after Susie.

"Wait for me!" she said. "We're a team, remember?"